# Secrets and Sidelines

## Rachelle Valentine

Never be afraid or ashamed of who you truly are.

# Trigger Warnings

Trigger warnings:

- Derogatory name calling/remarks in reference to sexual orientation (not between main characters). I do not condone the use of these terms in any way.

- Sexual assault

# Contents

# Prologue

Remember that rhyme you learned as a kid about how secrets can hurt someone? What about when a secret can help someone?

Lisa Lancaster has been my best friend since we were little. On my first day at my new school after my mom and I had moved, Lisa offered to be my friend, and we've been inseparable ever since. Her family treats me like one of their own. I'm always at her place, especially because my single mother works a lot. She's a great mom, and she does everything she can to make sure we don't go without. Unfortunately, that means working a lot of hours.

As usual, Lisa and I are hanging out at her house. I'm wearing my favorite comfy outfit of a crop top and shorts. Unlike most girls in high school, I actually love my body, so I don't mind showing it off a little.

After Lisa and I finish painting our nails, the front door opens, as Michael, my best friend's brother, walks in the house. We've all grown up together. Michael has always been like a brother to me. He's protected me like a big brother would, and he's even tried to scare away boys who try to cop a feel. He never complains when we want to hang out with him and his friends, and honestly, I think he'd rather spend the time with us.

When he passes by us, I get a good look and can see his eye is beginning to swell and turn purple.

"Oh my god! What happened?" Lisa asks.

Michael just shakes his head and heads towards his room.

Lisa immediately jumps off the couch to follow him, and I follow her. Michael's room is immaculately clean, as always.

Lisa opens his door without knocking

"Jesus Lisa, knock god damn it. I just want to be alone." Michael says.

"I don't think so. What the hell happened?"

"What do you think happened? The team happened."

"They did this to you?" Lisa asks as she gently places her hand on his swollen cheek.

"Yeah."

"Because of the rumors?"

"I mean we know they aren't rumors." He chuckles. I've known Michael was gay for as long as I can remember. He's never hidden it, well at least not around his family or myself. When we'd watch television shows and gush about the hot guy on screen, he'd chime in right along with us talking about the character's fine physique. He's never hidden it around us, but high school can be a cruel place. Everyone in high school sees the confident, sometimes cocky, quarterback. I see the vulnerable man underneath, just wanting to fit in.

"Still they can't treat you this way! We need to go to the coach immediately."

"Won't do any good. Trevor was the one who punched me, you know his old man won't do anything about it." Michael says with a shrug. "The guys already told Coach that they don't want me in the showers because they think I'm watching them. They say I'm making them uncomfortable."

"Then we'll go to the principal, the superintendent, someone!"

Michael shakes his head. "It won't do any good, sis. This town lives and breathes football, and hates anyone who's different."

"You can't just let them do this to you!" Lisa says with tears in her eyes.

"I don't know what else to do."

"What if you did a fake girlfriend thing?" Lisa asks, and Michael gives her an exasperated look. "It happens all the time in romance novels."

"You read romance novels?" Michael asks.

"Not the important part here." Lisa says.

"Nah, I couldn't do that. I wouldn't want to hurt the girl's feelings or get her hopes up. I also don't know anyone I would be able to trust enough. The whole point of the fake relationship would be so no one found out. If I can't trust the girl, then it would be pointless."

An idea comes to mind. "What if I help?" I ask.

Michael chuckles. "Grace, you know I love you like a sister, but what can you do to help? You gonna hit Trevor? You might break your pretty nails."

I scoff and then look down to my nails. Lisa and I did just finish painting them. *Not the point.* I think.

"There's that party tonight, right? At Trevor's house?"

"Yeah, what about it?"

"What if we went?" I ask.

"How would that help? I'd probably just get another fist to the jaw." Michael says.

"What if we went together?" I say.

"We always go everywhere together." Michael says, clearly not understanding what I'm suggesting.

Apparently Lisa gets it because she squeals. "Yes! This could definitely work."

"What could?" Michael asks, still confused.

"You and Grace go to the party, together, together." She says, wiggling her eyebrows in a suggestive manner.

"That would never work. The guys know she's like a little sister to me." Michael says, shaking his head.

"You two go to the party and dispel the rumors." Lisa continues.

"They'd never believe it." He says again.

"Then make them believe it. Kiss her if you have to."

"Excuse me, what? I was thinking about holding hands or something." I say shyly.

"That wouldn't work, you need something bigger to show you're really into each other." Lisa says.

Michael gives me a pleading look. "Please, Grace. I know this isn't fair to you, but it would really help me out."

Can I really do this? When I suggested it, I figured we could walk in holding hands, and everyone would buy it. They're right though, it wouldn't be enough. But having Michael be my first kiss? One neither of us would truly want? But then again, he's basically my brother, and I'd do anything for Lisa and her family.

"Okay, I'm in."

Michael comes over to me and wraps me in a hug. "Thank you! I'll never be able to repay you."

# CHAPTER 1



That rhyme... the one about secrets. Well it's not as simple as the rhyme made it seem. The rhyme never tells you that sometimes secrets can help, sometimes secrets are fun, and sometimes they hurt you more than you could ever realize, just by not being able to tell anyone the truth. I'm not just talking about being unable to share Michael's secret. That is one I will hold to myself forever, if I have to. Although, I see the toll it takes on him to keep himself hidden. I'm talking about my own secret, the one that has been tearing me up inside. The one I can't tell him, ever.

Michael was a year ahead of us in school and got a football scholarship, and Lisa and I decided to follow him to Crestview University. I had hoped that once we got to college, he would feel like he could be himself, his true self. However, he doesn't think that the other players on the football team will understand or accept him. I don't blame him for feeling this way, after everything that happened in high school, but from the guys I've met on the team, they actually seem pretty decent. So, we've kept up on our fake relationship.

When I first got to college, Michael asked if I wanted to stop our charade, so I could go out with other guys. He wanted to give me a chance to live, to feel free, which is extremely sweet of him since I know he doesn't feel free. He still feels the need to put on his mask.

Little does he know, I wear a mask of my own. I acted like we could continue the guise of our relationship for his sake, but that's not the whole truth.

I catch up with Lisa as we leave our class for the day, "Bachelorette tonight?" I ask.

"Sorry, I can't. I have a shift tonight." Lisa replies.

"You gonna be mad if Michael and I watch it without you?" I ask.

Lisa snickers. "No, I love my brother, but I don't need to hear him talk about how hot all the contestants are and what he would do with them if he was the one they were all fighting for."

"Like that time that he was talking about all the things he'd do in the fantasy suite?" I ask giggling.

Lisa fake gags. "Yeah, he has a more active imagination that I do, and I read a lot of smut."

I giggle at her antics, but she's right. I wave her off as she strides towards her job at the bookstore on campus.

As I walk towards Michael's dorm, I take note of the scene around me. There are quite a few people milling around after class. Some are throwing a football around, some are studying, and some are sitting and chatting.A lot of people probably think I'm a bitch because I keep to myself. I don't go out of my way to talk to people or make new friends.

I'm walking behind a girl who must not have been paying attention because she slips off the edge of the sidewalk and her books and papers go flying.

"Oh crap!" She states. As she's picking up her books, I rush around to try and catch her papers for her.

"Thank you so much! I need to pay better attention to where I'm going." She says. I give her a small understanding smile and turn to leave.

"Hey, you're Grace right?" She asks. I turn to get a good look at her, and I recognize her from one of my classes.

"Yeah." I say.

"Would you ever want to hang out? Get a coffee or study or anything?" She asks.

Dread fills my gut. "Um, thanks but no." I say as I scurry off. *Exactly why people think you're a bitch,* I think to myself.

As I finally get to Michael's room, I knock. I haven't met his new roommate yet, and I don't want to just barge in, just in case Michael isn't there. Michael comes to open the door for me with a big smile on his face.

"Bachelorette night." He says. I smirk as I guide past him. Watching the Bachelorette, with Lisa, has always been our thing. We always talk about who the most attractive guy is and bet on who's going to win. His room is a little larger than most typical dorms. I'm guessing it's because athletes, as they do in most places, get a little bit of preferential treatment. The room is basically divided into two sides with beds on either end and a couch and television taking up the middle. Michael's side of the room is exceptionally clean, as usual.

As I settle into the couch, Michael surprises me by saying, "You know we can stop this whenever you want."

"What?"

"I just don't see what you're getting out of it. You've been helping me with this for years now. Don't you want to go out? Party? Hook-up? Date?" He asks.

I shake my head and control the shiver that is coursing through me. I couldn't imagine putting myself out there like that. Not after what happened.

Trying to play it off, I say. "Why would I want to date, when I've got you."

He scoffs. "It's not like I can give you what you need, Grace."

"And what do you think I need?"

"An orgasm?" He asks and I scoff.

He chuckles. "Okay, how about a connection with someone. Romantic feelings. Love."

"When you find love, I'll go try to find it for myself." I say.

"It's not the same Grace. I can't go find love. I don't want to be treated that way again." He says solemnly.

"It's college, Michael. It's a time where everyone explores themselves, finds out who they truly are. You've known who you were since we were younger. Why can't you just show other people how amazing you are? Regardless of who you love."

"I wish I could." He says. After a couple of minutes of silence, he says, "But it's different for you. If it weren't for me, you could be out meeting people, guys or girls if that's your preference." He winks and I roll my eyes.

"I've told you before, I'm not attracted to women like that. I just don't want to date anyone right now."

"I just don't get it. If I could, I would be dating, hooking-up, all the things people associate with college."

"You do hook up." I remind him.

He chuckles. "Yeah, but only you and I know that. Seriously though, I worry about you. Did something happen? I mean you've changed a lot since high school. I'm not saying it's a bad thing, you're still amazing. You're just more introverted and your clothing style has changed. I mean why are you so anti-men?"

I still. I can't tell him. Not like it would matter anyway, but I just can't. Not yet, and maybe not ever.

"I just don't need a man." I reply.

"Don't you want to be happy?"

"I am happy." I say defensively.

"I mean really happy. I know you don't need a partner to be happy, but I know Lisa and I are basically the only two people you talk to. You need to be able to experience all that college has to offer. You need to be young, have fun."

I want to argue, but he's right. I don't go out, party, date, or any of it. I just can't, and I can't explain why. Not to him.

"Again, when you find love and are able to be happy yourself, I'll think about it." I say.

He sighs. He's known me long enough to know that he can only try to argue with me so much.

Luckily, the conversation is interrupted when his door suddenly opens and in walks the sexiest man I've ever seen.

He has dark black hair and stunning blue eyes. Eyes that remind me of the ocean the day of a storm. They're depths are dragging me in like the force of a tidal wave. From his muscular build, I'd guess he was also on the football team. I feel my panties dampening, something that doesn't happen to me. I try to avoid men like the plague, partially why my understanding with Michael works out so well.

"Oh shit, sorry man. I didn't know you had someone here. Next time, put a sock on the door or something." The mysterious sexy man says.

Michael chuckles. "Sorry about that, just spending some time with my girl."

I turn back to look at the mystery man, who I assume is Michael's roommate, who is looking at me just as intensely. Does he feel this same strange connection that I do?

He runs a hand through his hair. What I wouldn't give to run my hand through it. It looks so soft.

"Yeah.... I'll just come back then. Sorry man."

And just like that, he's gone.

"Who was that?"

"Oh that's Nolan, he plays defense, inside linebacker. He transferred here this year." Michael says.

Funny, I would've guessed tight end. Apparently, that little comment I thought I kept to myself slips out.

"Hot right?" Michael says. Then he sighs. "Too bad he doesn't play for my team."

"He's not on the football team?"

Michael just shakes his head. "Oh poor sweet innocent little Grace. I mean he's straight."

I blush. "Oh."

"Damn, we really need to get you laid." He chuckles.

I swat him on the chest. "How do you know I haven't?" I say and my insides clench. Michael doesn't know the secret I have. The one I've hidden from him since high school. I hope he never finds out. It's the reason I've kept up with our charade as long as I have, well that and I'd do absolutely anything for Lisa and Michael. It's the reason I avoid men, well straight men I guess.

"Oh I know. You've been pretending with me for years. When would you have had time? Not that I'd blame you for sneaking around on me." He winks.

"You haven't told him?" I ask, trying to change the subject.

"Nah, he's a nice guy and all, but I don't want it getting around the team. That's why I have you." He says as he nudges my shoulder.

# Chapter 2

What the hell is wrong with me? Am I lusting after my roommate's girlfriend? I had seen her around campus before, but I never knew she was seeing Michael. Just the other day, I spotted her helping another student pick up her papers that went flying around after she mis stepped off the sidewalk. The week before, she paid for someone's lunch who forgot their wallet. I was impressed by her kindness to help someone that she didn't know. Most of the times that I saw her I was running late to one class or another, or she didn't seem to want to be bothered, so I hadn't made that move. Which now, I am extremely grateful for.

Seeing her in her oversized sweatshirt and leggings hanging around in my room did something to me the other day. She wasn't like the other girls on campus who are constantly trying to show as much skin as possible. I haven't been able to stop thinking about her since. Just one look at her long brown hair and gorgeous hazel eyes, I was hooked. When I looked into her eyes, I swear I saw pain in their depths. However, there was something else I saw in them, it was like a deep connection was forming. I wanted to get closer to see if they had more green, more brown, or more blue inside them. There's no way she felt it too though, even though for a moment I thought she did. She's with

Michael for goodness sake. And Michael's a great guy, I really lucked out getting him for a roommate.

When I first met him though, I thought he was gay. He's a hugger. I've gotten plenty of hugs in my life from my family, but teammates are more likely to smack your shoulder, give you a fist bump, hell, even smack your ass. Then his side of the room is always so clean, meticulously so. Not that straight men aren't clean, but he seems to take it to an extreme. I know these are not solid pieces of evidence of him preferring to be with men, but it was just where my brain went. Stereotypes are a bitch to overcome. I wouldn't care if he was, growing up my parents always taught me to accept everyone as they are.

"Hey man." Michael says as he enters the locker room before our game.

"Hey." I reply.

"Stats just came out. We are crushing our division man. I know we'll definitely make it to the championship." Michael says with a smile. "I mean, have you seen our quarterback?" He winks.

I roll my eyes, but he isn't wrong. Michael is an amazing quarterback. I know he broke quite a few records in high school, and he's on his way to doing it again here. Not to toot my own horn, but our defensive line is a force to be reckoned with as well.

"We both know the defensive line is the reason we're doing so well." I joke.

"Yeah yeah, they're okay." He says with an eye roll and a smirk. "You still happy you transferred?"

"Absolutely. The other college was too far away from my family. We've always been close. When I got offered the scholarship here, I couldn't turn it down. "

"How was the football program there?"

"Not bad, we would have crushed them though." I say.

After we're both suited up, Michael smacks my shoulder. "Ready for this?" He asks.

"Born ready." I say.

The team walks out of the tunnel and runs onto the field. The rush of the game fills me with adrenaline. I've always loved football. I felt that it gave me another family, a sense of belonging. As with any sport, there are some of my teammates that are rough around the edges, but for the most part, my teammates are great.

I'm standing next to Michael when I see a huge smile take over his face. I turn to look at what he's looking at, and I see her, Grace. She's wearing Michael's jersey and sitting next to his sister, Lisa, who I've met quite a few times. It makes me an asshole to admit, but seeing her in his jersey is like a punch to the gut. I'd much rather her be wearing my jersey, be here cheering for me. God, I'm a dick. How can I even think of her like that when Michael has been nothing but nice to me. Regardless of how I'm feeling, I'll never act on it. I've never cheated on a woman, and I won't be a homewrecker.

"She your good luck charm?" I ask.

"Always." He says with that dopey smile. "She was always at my games in high school, even before we got together because she would come with Lisa. Since then, she's been a constant for me. Always in the stands cheering the team on."

Jealousy flairs through me. *Take it out on the field.* I tell myself

She makes eye contact with me, and her eyes go wide. I swear a blush covers her cheeks.

I should turn around, but my momma raised me to never be rude, so I give her a small wave, probably looking like an idiot in the process.

I turn back to the field to bring myself back into the game. I can't afford distractions.

The game starts off strong. Michael's arm is on fire. We're already up 17-0. As the offensive line is coming in, I see Michael winking towards where Grace is sitting. It hits something deep inside me, causing way too many feelings to swell through me.

I take a deep breath as I line up on the defensive line, waiting for the snap of the ball. My eyes are burning through the snapper, watching every twitch of his fingers as he waits to release the ball. As soon as he does, I'm off. Honestly, I'm surprised they don't call offsides because of how fast I'm moving.

I take off towards the quarterback. He doesn't even have a moment to find an open receiver before I'm on him. He falls to the ground and by pure luck, he loses his grasp on the ball, causing a fumble. My teammates weren't as quick to get over here, so on pure adrenaline, I push off the quarterback and snatch the ball.

Then I'm off, hurtling myself towards our end zone. I'm running faster than I think I ever have in my life. I'm channeling all my feelings into pushing my legs faster. All the confusion, jealousy, anger, it's all propelling me forward.

I arrive in the endzone easily as the ref's blow their whistles signaling a touchdown. My teammates rally around me pushing and smacking me in their excitement. I'm breathing heavily, but I have a huge smile adorning my face. What a rush.

As the defensive line scurries back to the sidelines, while we wait for the special teams to attempt the extra points, my coach grabs me by my facemask.

"Holy shit Carver! I don't know what's gotten into you today but keep it up!" He says as he slaps me on the back.

Michael walks over and gives me a huge hug. As always, I give him a pat on the back as he brings me in.

"Hell of a play, Carver."

"Thanks man."

The rest of the game flies by. Michael keeps throwing unbelievable passes, getting us two more touchdowns. The defense and I keep busting ass to keep them from scoring. The final score is 37-0. The locker room is loud as the players are all cheering because of the win. While inside, I'm torn. I'm happy we won, and I had a great game. However, I still don't have what I want, her. As awful as that is, wanting your best friend's girl. So many emotions are raging through me, elation, jealousy, guilt. I hate feeling this way.

As I walk out of the locker room, getting ready to go back to my dorm, I'm stopped by my parents.

"Good game son." My dad says as he pats me on the back. My mom gives me a big hug.

"We're so proud of you." Mom says.

"Thanks." I say.

"You okay, honey? You don't seem as happy as I thought you'd be." She says. She never misses anything. I shrug.

"How about we go get something to eat. I'm sure you're starving." She says.

"Sure mom. That sounds great." I say.

As we start to walk out to the parking lot, I spot Grace. She's standing with Lisa, probably waiting for Michael. She looks towards me, and a blush crosses her cheeks again. I duck my head, trying to keep the smile off my face.

My mom, as perceptive as ever, looks at me out of the corner of her eye.

When we arrive at a local diner, after ordering, my mom finally breaks the ice. "So... who was that?"

"Who was who?" I ask.

"Nolan, don't play coy with me. The girl you were making googly eyes at."

I chuckle. "Googly eyes, really mom?"

"What? I'm just calling it as I see it. You were like that emoticon with heart eyes."

"You mean emoji?" I say chuckling again.

"Whatever, you knew what I meant."

"That was Grace."

"And who is this Grace?" Her eyes lighting up, like I've told her that I've found the one woman I wanted to spend the rest of my life with.

"My roommate's girlfriend." I say.

"Oh." My mother softly whispers. "Okay, I was not expecting that."

"Yeah, me either."

"Do you like her?" My mother asks.

"Does that matter?" I retort.

"Son, I know you're a good kid and a good man." My father says. "I know you'd never do something to intentionally hurt someone or break up a relationship."

"You're right, I wouldn't." I say.

"Good." He says with a nod of his head. "I'm glad I raised you right."

"You did." I say with a sigh.

"Life isn't always fair, Nolan. Sometimes things are put into your life that you can't have, and once you realize that, you find something even better waiting for you." My mom says.

As silly as it sounds though, I don't think I could find anything better than Grace though. We don't know each other super well, but I know enough. Now, yes, most of my information is from stories I've heard from Michael, which makes this whole situation even worse.

But I know she's smart, she's beautiful, and she is without a doubt one of the kindest people I've ever met. Her heart, that enough would make anyone fall in love with her.

"And sometimes... things are put into your life for a reason. Even though it's not the right time or place, maybe it just isn't your time.... yet." She says with a simple shrug and goes back to eating.

I would never betray Michael and try to steal her from him. He's just as kind as she is. That doesn't mean that I can't hope that someday she can be mine. I'm sure I should listen to my mom's other piece of advice and realize I can't have her and move on. I just can't, not yet. I haven't looked at other women at all since I've met her. No one's caught my attention the way she has. However, I know, deep down, that if she and Michael are truly happy with each other and stay together. I won't do anything to get in their way, even if it breaks my own heart in the process.

# Chapter 3

I've been meeting with the school counselor ever since I started college. I've never told Michael, but Lisa knows. She knows everything.

"So how have you been Grace?" Ms. Lisbon asks.

"Same old." I reply.

"You know, if you really want to work past your trauma, you're going to have to open up to me a little more during our sessions."

I sigh, knowing she's right.

"Have you spent any time with anyone outside of Lisa and Michael?" She asks.

I fiddle with the hem of my shirt. "No."

"We've talked about this Grace, you need to meet new people. That's part of what college is about, getting out there, meeting new people."

"Hey, I talked to someone a few days ago." I retort.

"Oh yeah? Tell me about it." My counselor says.

"Well, a girl had dropped her books and papers and I chased them around to pick them up for her. Then she asked me to get coffee or study with her sometime."

"That was very nice of you to help her. What did you say to her question?" She asked, as I turned my head so she couldn't see the blush appear on my face confirming that she was right.

"Mmm."

"I know... I just..." I sigh. "A lot of ways that people meet or hang out in college are at parties, and I just don't know if I'm ready to go to one."

"I understand that it might cause some of your memories to re-emerge or might trigger you, but I don't think it's healthy to hole yourself up either." She says. "How about you start with just having a conversation with someone you don't really know?"

"I can try." I say, and she nods like she doesn't believe me anymore than I believe myself.

"How is everything going with Michael?" She asks, trying to change the subject, which I'm grateful for.

"Michael brought up again about ending our arrangement." I say.

"And how does that make you feel?"

I glare at her. I hate that question, and she knows it. It's so cliche.

She chuckles. "Sorry, does that make you feel good or bad?"

"I don't want it to end. It's helping him. I hate that he feels like he can't be himself though. I want him to be happy. I want him to be able to find someone, even if the rest of the world doesn't deem them as appropriate."

"And what about you?" She asks.

"What about me?"

Now I think she's the one glaring. "When are you going to go out and make yourself happy?"

The memories start to overwhelm me, and I feel tears pricking at my eyes. "I can't.... Not.... not yet."

"Look, Grace, I can't imagine what you went through, and I'm sure that you still carry some of that pain to this day, but you deserve happiness just as much as Michael does."

"I know." I whisper. If only it were that easy.

"So what happens when it does end?" She asks.

"What do you mean?"

"I mean, what happens to you? You're an amazing person with such a big heart. You've done this whole charade to help a friend in need. So, when this ends, and Michael is finally free to be himself and possibly finds love. Where does that leave you?"

"I don't know." I croak.

"Well, I think it is something that you need to think about. I think that you have hidden all your emotions and have always had Michael to fall back on. However, there will come a point where this ends. Yes, you'll still be friends, but I'm sure you wouldn't spend as much time together. So, I want you to think about what it is you truly want for your life. After Michael, after college. What would make you happy?"

I hate to admit that she's right. Michael has been my buffer. I haven't had to worry about boys, heartbreak, or anything of the sort because I had Michael and our pretend love.

I nod and tell her that I'll see her next week.

After the emotionally draining counseling session, all I want to do is relax with Michael and watch the Bachelorette. However, when I go to Michael's room and the door opens, it's not Michael, it's Nolan.

I can feel the blush cover my cheeks. "Um, hi. Sorry, I was hoping Michael was here." I say.

"Offensive line had an extended practice today." Nolan says. "Do you want to come in and wait?"

I probably shouldn't, the feelings I have for Nolan are conflicting. I don't get butterflies from being around boys, I typically feel nauseous, and I definitely don't start getting wet down there. I know I should probably just tell him to have Michael call me. For some reason though, I nod and walk in.

As I make my way towards their couch, feeling a bit uneasy, not because of Nolan though. For some reason, he makes me feel safe and comfortable. I plop down with a sigh.

"Everything alright?" Nolan asks.

"Yep." I all but squeak. *Get it together!*

The silence stretches on, and I can feel this weird sensation in my stomach. I'm not really sure what to say. The only people I ever talk to are Lisa and Michael, but I can do this, even if it's just to tell my counselor about it next week and prove her wrong.

"I'm sorry, I'm not good at talking to people. I'm mostly an introvert, I guess. The only people I really talk to are Lisa and Michael."

"Have you two been together for a long time?" Nolan asks.

"We all three grew up together. They're home was basically my home. I grew up with a single mother. She was great, but she had to work a lot to provide for us. I spent most of my time at Michael's home." I say with a smile.

"That's nice that you had that." He says.

"Yeah, his parents are great. They always welcomed me. I had dinner with them almost every night, usually spent the weekends there too."

"Wow, his parents were cool with that, with you two being together?"

Well since they knew their son was definitely not attracted to me like that, yes, they were more than fine with it. I can't say that to Nolan though. I can't betray Michael, I would never. Not even for the hottest man I've ever seen.

"We were good kids. I would stay with Lisa in her room, obviously. His parents trusted us." I say and Nolan nods. Hopefully that was believable. "What about you? What was your family like?"

"My family is great. I have a younger brother, Noah. My parents are both super supportive of both of us. We had family dinner together every night." He says with a smile.

"They sound amazing. Do they come to many of your games?" I ask.

"As many as they can. They live about two hours away." He says. "They were part of the reason I decided to transfer here. It was closer to home."

"Where did you go before this?"

"A college in Florida. They offered a great scholarship. At first, I thought it would be great to get away, but I realized it was just too far from my family."

It's so sweet how much he loves his family. When I was younger and pictured a man that I wanted, he was a family man. I had always wanted a larger family, and I wanted a man who was close to his family. Nothing against my mom, she was great, and she did everything she could for me, but I'd be lying if it wasn't lonely at times.

"When did you start playing football?" I ask.

A huge smile overtakes his face. "I've been playing ever since I was little. It was all I wanted to do when I was younger. My dad swears I'm the reason he's got a bad shoulder now." He says with a chuckle.

"You did really good last week." I say.

"Thanks. It was a good game. The team was on fire. Michael's got a hell of an arm." He says. He's so humble, another thing I'm not entirely used to in football players. Obviously, Michael is humble, but most of the football players at our high school were arrogant, rude, and just downright assholes. I'm surprised to see that players in college, who are more talented than the boys from my high school could ever be, aren't preening in the spotlight. Instead, Nolan is talking about the team as a whole. He looks so proud of them as he talks about them.

The awkward silence begins to fill the room again, and as much as I don't typically socialize with people, I hate silence. It unnerves me.

"So you already know I'm more of an introvert, but awkward silences kill me. What else should we talk about?" I ask.

Nolan chuckles. "We can talk about anything. We've already talked about our families. School would be a safe topic to start with. What's your major?"

"Undecided right now. I'm just taking the essential classes until I figure out what I really want to do."

"That's smart. How are your classes going?"

"Good. I've always excelled in school. What about your, what's your major?"

"When I was younger, I wanted to go pro football. That's still a dream of mine, but I also want to make sure that I have a good education and a backup plan in case that doesn't work out. I don't know if I'll get drafted, and even if I do, injuries can happen at any moment. So, I'm majoring in sports medicine."

"Wow, that's awesome. Smart, to have that plan, but I don't think you'll have any problems finding a team who wants you."

I swear he blushes. "Thanks."

"How are your classes going?" I ask, and he just stares at me for a minute. Is that a sensitive question? Why is he looking at me like he didn't understand it?

"Um, actually I'm struggling a bit in psychology." He says as he rubs the back of his neck.

"Really? I'm in Psychology 302 right now, which class are you in?"

"Psychology 201."

"I took that one last year. It was really informative." I say.

"Do you..." He pauses to clear his throat. "Do you think you could help me with some of the theories?"

"Umm…" I start, unsure of what to say. I like helping people, really, I do, but that would also mean being alone with him, which is a bad idea. Although, not for the reason I expect. I expected to feel uncomfortable, but that isn't at all what I'm feeling. Instead, it's like butterflies are swirling in my stomach. "Sure?"

"Thanks, Grace." He says with a soft smile.

Just then Michael comes in.

"Man, that was rough, Coach is definitely trying to kill us." Michael says as he drops his bag to the floor. Then he notices me.

"Hey Grace, I didn't know you were coming over." He says as he makes his way to me and brings me off the couch and in for a hug.

I look to Nolan, but he darts his eyes away.

"How was practice?" I ask.

"Grueling. Glad you're here." He says as he sits down with me.

"Um, I'm just gonna give you guys some space." Nolan says.

"Dude, you don't have to. It's not like we're gonna get naked or anything." Michael says with a chuckle. When I look at Nolan, I can't decipher the emotion that crosses his eyes.

# CHAPTER 4

Why did I lie about struggling with Psychology? I'm a good student. What the hell is wrong with me? I don't even have time for extra study sessions. I'm already feeling maxed out between football and my studies, which I'm doing perfectly fine in. *You wanted to spend more time with her,* my traitorous brain reminds me.

Then on top of that lie, I had to lie to Michael.

"Can I ask you something?" Michael asks.

"Sure, what's up?"

"Why did you ask her for help with your studies? From what I've seen on all your papers, you're getting straight A's in your classes."

*Shit. Busted.*

"I'm doing well in all of my other classes, but psychology messes with me. The theories are all so confusing to keep straight. Also, didn't you say Grace needed to work on talking to people who aren't you and your sister?"

He looks at me skeptically, but for some reason, doesn't call me out on my apparent bullshit.

"Well I hope she can help you figure out the theories. I could never keep them straight either."

My parents always taught me about the value of honesty and how important it is to all friendships and relationships. I'm better than this, than lying and deceiving people.


As I'm walking to the student center, where Grace and I decided to meet, I'm telling myself that I need to be honest with her and call this whole thing off. It's not fair to her to waste her time on someone who doesn't actually need help. It also just isn't right.

When I get inside the student center, it is buzzing with students. Some are eating, some are chatting, some are studying, but there are a lot of people here. When I find Grace sitting at a table in the corner, I forget everything I had told myself in my pep talk walking over here. I want this time with her, even if it's wrong.

"Hey." I say as I sit down with my bookbag.

"Hey." She squeaks.

"Ready to get started?" I ask.

"Sure. What part of the coursework are you struggling the most with?" She asks, but she isn't making eye contact with me. She's looking around at everyone else.

"I just keep getting the theories confused." I say, reiterating the lie I told Michael.

"Okay, well we can start with the most well known and then work our way through some of the others."

"Thanks. That would be great."

As we start talking about Freud and Skinner, I notice that she looks uncomfortable. I'm terrified that it's me making her feel that way.

"You okay?" I ask.

"Yep." She says in a rather high pitched voice.

"You look like you're ready to bolt. I'm sorry if I'm doing something to make you uncomfortable."

She sighs. "It's not you. I just don't do well in crowds. Heck, it took a lot out of me to just talk with you."

There's so much I want to ask her. I want to find out why she doesn't like crowds, why she doesn't surround herself with anyone other than Michael and Lisa, why she's so shy and introverted, but how do you just ask someone that? Obviously, something has happened in her past to make her this way. We may be sitting here together, but it's not like we're friends, or more than friends if I had it my way.

"Can I ask why you agreed to this then?" I ask, hoping it's a safe enough question.

She blushes a bit. "My counselor said that I should talk to more people, it was kind of like my homework from her."

So whatever she's endured was traumatic enough to put her into counseling. For some reason, that irritates me. I don't think it was her family because when we talked about families, she didn't complain about her single mom working a lot. She seemed to be understanding of it. What could have happened to this girl to make her so nervous?

She interrupts my thoughts when she says, "I probably shouldn't have said that."

"Why?"

"Because people look down on other people when they say they're in counseling. They're either looked at as weak or literally crazy."

"I don't think you're weak or crazy. I also don't think that there's anything wrong with needing someone to talk to. Don't ever feel embarrassed about getting counseling. If it's helping you to deal with things, whatever they may be, then it doesn't matter what anyone else thinks." I say.

"Thanks." She says as she tucks a piece of her brown locks behind her ear.

"Are you ready to continue, or do you want to call it a night?" I ask because I don't want her to feel any more uncomfortable than she already is.

"We can keep going for a little bit longer." She says with a small smile.

We continue talking about different theorists and their theories, all of which I know, but I try to ask questions to sell my lie. All while it's eating away inside of me. *This isn't me.* After about a half an hour has passed, and she begins to pack her things, I know I need to tell her.

Instead of blurting out the truth that I don't need the tutoring or taking an easier way out and saying that she's already helped me so much we don't need to continue, I say "How about next time we meet at the library in one of the study rooms, that way there won't be as many people."

She looks at me with what almost looks like unshed tears in her eyes. "That would be great. Thank you for thinking of me."

I nod, and as I escort her out of the building, I feel that guilt overwhelming me. Once I wave goodbye to her, I decide to take the long way back to my dorm to try and figure out what the hell I'm supposed to do now. The morally right thing would be to tell her the truth, that I don't need help, but then how would I explain that I asked her for help in the first place?

*Even though you're dating my roommate and teammate, I still wanted to spend alone time with you, but I'd never intentionally come between you two and break you up.*

Yeah, that sounds like a disaster waiting to happen. How did I get myself into this mess? My parents taught me better. I know better. I don't lie. I mean I'm sure I did as a kid, who didn't. I'm not perfect, but I'm not this person.

"I did it." I say proudly.

"Did what?" Ms. Lisbon asks.

"I talked to someone new."

She looks shocked for a minute; she probably didn't believe I would actually take her advice. I can't blame her.

"Okay, tell me about it. Who was it?"

"Michael's roommate."

"And what did you talk about?"

"We talked about families, and then he asked me to help him with his studies for psychology."

"And what did you say?"

"I agreed."

"Really?" She asks.

I roll my eyes. "Don't try to act so shocked when I actually take your advice."

She chuckles. "Sorry, it's just that you typically find a loophole for my advice or just don't do it at all."

I shrug, knowing she isn't wrong. "Have you started the study sessions?"

"Yes."

"And how are they going?"

"Good..." I say but draw the word out.

"Why do you say it like that?"

"Well, I guess I'm just confused. Nolan is very smart. I don't really understand why he needs help. He picks up the theories really well."

"Hmm." She hums instead of actually responding.

"How do you fe.." She starts but changes her wording it when I give her a glare. "How is it going being alone with him?"

"Actually, it hasn't been too bad."

"Hmm." She responds again.

"Okay, seriously? What does that mean, hmm?"

"Nothing." She says, as I roll my eyes again.

"So, do you think you'd be ready to try and get out there? Meeting someone new and going for coffee or going to a party perhaps?" Ms. Lisbon asks.

"I don't know if I'm ready for that yet."

"I don't want to push you, and I am really proud of this step for you. Just think about it. Eventually, you'll have to get back out there."

"Hmm." I respond.

She chuckles again. "Touche."

I'm thrumming with energy as I wait for Nolan and our second study session. I'm thankful he agreed to do this in the library's study room, so that I'm not surrounded by people.

He looks so good when he walks in, dressed in sweatpants that show his fit legs and a fitted t-shirt that is pulled tight over his muscles. His hair is unruly and still looks to be wet, like he just got out of the shower.

"Sorry I'm a couple minutes late. I had to shower after practice, didn't want to stink up the place."

"No problem. Ready to get started?" I ask, and he nods.

As we go through some of the major psychologists and their theories, I'm beginning to think I was right in doubting that Nolan needs a tutor.

"So, what is a summary of Erikson's classical conditioning theory?" I ask, seeing if he'll catch it and my suspicions are correct.

"You mean Pavlov?" He responds. *Bingo.* This guy doesn't need help at all in psychology. So again, why is he doing this?

"Oh, oops, slip of the tongue, I guess." I want to call him out, ask him why he's pretending. Is this a game to him? Did Michael ask him to talk to me because I don't talk to many people, and he took pity on me?

Instead of any of those things coming out of my mouth, I ask. "What is something you don't like about football?"

Nolan looks taken aback for a minute but then chuckles. "Random, but okay. Even though I'm on the defensive line, I've never really been an aggressive person. I hate the idea of hurting someone."

"So why didn't you join the offensive line or the special teams?" I ask. He stops and just stares at me for a moment.

"What?" I ask, when again, the silence becomes too much.

"Sorry. I'm just not used to girls knowing things about football, no offense."

I smirk. "None taken, but you do realize that I'm dating a football player. Have been for a while, it'd be rude not to learn something along the way."

His face seems to fall for a moment, but then he pastes on a smile. "Yeah, I guess you'd be able to pick up a thing or two. Okay, let me think of something equally random." He says as he taps his finger to his chin. "What's your favorite food?"

"Mexican food." I say with a smile. "That was one of the traditions my mom and I always had. Even with her busy schedule, she would always make the time to take me to a Mexican restaurant for dinner, usually once a month. The food is delicious, and it brings back good memories."

"So are you dating anyone?" I ask and then want to face palm myself. It's not my business, and it's not like I can do anything about it anyways. "Sorry, I shouldn't have asked that."

"Nah, I've got a lot going on with school and football. I don't have time for a girlfriend." He says.

I deflate. He didn't strike me as a player, but I know most athletes are. Sorry to stereotype, but from what I've seen, they mostly hit it and quit it. Competing to see who has the most notches on their bed posts.

"I'm not a player either." He says as if he's reading my mind. "I've been with girls, sure, but I'm not like some of the stereotypical jocks. I like women, but I respect them too." He says, causing me to swoon.

"So, you're perfect then?" I ask before my brain catches up to whatever the hell my mouth is deciding to spew. "Oh my gosh, pretend I didn't say that." *This is why I shouldn't talk to people.*

As my cheeks flush from embarrassment, he smiles. "Not perfect. I've got plenty of flaws."

"Oh yeah? Like what. From what I'm seeing, you're humble, re-spectful, come from a good family, and are easy on the eyes." *Okay mouth you can shut up at any time now.*

"I'm easy on the eyes, huh?"

When I turn to him, he's looking at me, that same intense look that he had when I first met him. His look sends tingles throughout my body and heat to my core. I want him to kiss me so badly. Our faces seem to be moving just a bit closer to each other.

"I can't do this." He whispers. "I shouldn't want you like this. You're with Michael."

I want to tell him the truth, but it isn't my secret to tell. I can't do that to Michael, even if I want this man more than I've ever wanted anyone in my life.

"You're right. I can't do this to Michael. I'm sorry." I say as tears well in my eyes. I grab my things and run from the room.

# CHAPTER 5

*Grace*

It may be time for me to stop listening to my counselor. First, it was my awkward tutoring session with Nolan that ended with me running out of there like my butt was on fire. Now, I'm on my way to a frat party with Lisa.

Ever since high school, I haven't gone to parties. Too many potential triggers, and too many people. With my counselor's advice in my head though, I figured if I was going to try and meet and talk to new people, it would be safest to do it with my bestie by my side. My legs are trembling, as I walk arms linked with Lisa, and it's not just from the cold that's starting to settle into the air.

Lisa refused to let me wear my typical oversized hoodie tonight. Instead, I'm wearing leggings and a baggy sweater, which to me is the same concept but is apparently it is Lisa approved for a night out. She helped me do my makeup, which I never typically wear, and she helped me curl my hair.

As we start walking up the stairs to the frat house though, I'm starting to regret it. Coffee definitely would've been an easier start.

"'I'm surprised that you agreed to this. I'm proud of you though for coming." Lisa says.

"My counselor suggested I try meeting new people." I say while my nose scrunches up.

"It's not a bad thought. We don't have to stay long; I don't want you to feel even more uncomfortable." She grabs my hand and gives it a squeeze.

As we walk through the front door, my nostrils are filled with the scent of beer and sweat. There are so many people here. I may go to football games where there are a lot of people in the stands, but they're spread out and I don't have to talk to anyone. I can just be another face in an endless crowd. This is overwhelming.

After making our way through the horde of drunk college students, we find Michael and some of the football team in the kitchen by the drinks. I refuse to drink anything that I don't open myself, after last time. Lisa, knowing this, finds two unopened beer bottles and hands me one. I'm definitely going to need some kind of liquid courage to make it through tonight. I look around the kitchen and find Nolan. He looks amazing in his white button up shirt and dark wash jeans. His gaze meets mine, and he gives me a small smirk. The dang butterflies start fluttering around like crazy again.

I need to get away from him, just for a moment. I grab Lisa's hand, and I start pulling her towards another area of the house. That is, until I hear a guy's voice behind me, and I still. It sounds like Trevor, but there's no way he'd be here. He goes to Mentor College, which is an hour or so away. My mind is tricking me because of the atmosphere I'm in. Lisa senses my discomfort and turns to where the voice is coming from.

"Shit." Lisa says, her face paling.

As much as my head screams that this is a bad idea, I turn to look, and there he is, Trevor Donovan.

My body shuts down. My vision starts to spot, and my breath is coming out in short spurts.

"Shit, Michael!" I hear Lisa shout, but it sounds so far away, so distorted. I feel hands on me, rubbing my arms, trying to comfort me.

"No shit? Grace and Michael?" Trevor says with a chuckle. "I thought the whole thing in high school was fake. You two are still together?"

"What the fuck are you doing here Trevor?" Lisa asks.

"My cousin goes here and invited me to a party. You know I love my parties. Isn't that right, Gracie girl?" Trevor says with a wink. Then he gets closer and whispers, "We can have a repeat of our last party together."

I'm visibly trembling now. I feel like I'm drowning, unable to get any air in my lungs. I'm having another panic attack. If I live through this one, I need to talk to Ms. Lisbon about getting me on some kind of medication again.

"Grace, come on. Let's get out of here." Lisa says, but I can't move. It's just like all those years ago.

*I'm being carried up the stairs in a fireman's hold. I don't know who's carrying me. My brain feels foggy. This isn't the first time I've drank. Lisa, Michael, and I would sneak their parents' alcohol out of their cabinets, but I've never felt like this.*

*I'm thrown onto something soft. A bed, maybe? It feels comfy. My body feels sluggish, like I don't even have the energy to move. I open my eyes, and everything is blurry. What is happening to me?*

*"Gracie girl." I hear. I think it's Trevor's voice, but I can't be sure. "You must be a pretty good lay if even a queer gets between these thighs."*

*I've always known Trevor to be a bastard. The way he's made Michael's life a living hell. The derogatory way he's talking about Michael makes me sick. I hope I don't throw up though, I don't have the strength to move, and I'd hate to vomit all over myself or choke on it.*

*"What do you say boys? Should we take our turn too?"*

*Boys? Who the hell else is in here? Why can't I move to look around?*

*I hear what sounds like the ripping of plastic, and then I feel someone's weight on top of me.*

*No.. No.. No! I try to scream, but I feel too weak. I want to fight, but my body doesn't move. Then I feel the sharp pain coming from between my legs. Tears start rolling down my cheeks. After what feels like hours, the weight is gone. Just when I'm hopeful that my nightmare is over, I feel weight on top of me again. This continues a couple times, until I black out completely.*

Someone grabs my hand forcefully, bringing me out of the flashback. I start to fight whoever is holding my hand, fearful that it's Trevor.

"Hey, it's okay. I've got you." Nolan says as he cups my face. I look into his blue eyes, that remind me of an ocean during a storm, and my breathing starts to slow.

"What the fuck, man?" I hear Michael shouting in the kitchen.

"Come on, let's get out of here." Nolan says as he regrips my hand and pulls me towards the door.

Lisa runs out behind us. "Shit, Grace. Are you okay? I had no idea Trevor would be here or I would've never..."

I interrupt her. "I'm.... okay."

I hear footsteps behind us, and then arms wrap around my waist.

"Grace, what the fuck was that?" Michael says.

"I'll tell you later." Lisa says to him.

"No, I want to know right the fuck now. No more secrets. I know something happened in high school, but for her to have a reaction like that..." He trails off. "Tell me, now."

"Can... we.... not do this here, please?" I ask.

Michael looks at me and his eyes soften from the rage I see behind them. "Yeah, come on. Let's all go back to my room. But don't think you're getting out of this. I want to know what happened, the truth, all of it."

Once we arrive back at Michael and Nolan's room, and I sit down on the couch and close my eyes. I take a deep breath. I had hoped that I would never have to tell Michael the truth, that he would never find out. He already had enough problems with the football team, and I didn't want to add to them. Football is the only thing that has ever made him happy.

"I'm going to give you guys some time to talk. I'll be outside, let me know if you need anything." Nolan says and then leaves the room.

"Tell me what the hell is going on." Michael demands once the door closes.

Lisa looks towards me, I'm sure she's wanting my approval to start talking. I swore her to secrecy in high school. She had begged me to tell Michael, to tell someone, but I knew it wouldn't do any good.

"I..." I try to start but I get choked up, tears begin pouring down my face again.

"They raped her, Michael." Lisa softly says.

His mouth drops open. Then his eyes fill with rage.

"What the fuck do you mean?" He asks slowly.

I drop my head, unable to look at them.

"The night of one of Trevor's parties.." I start and take a deep breath to continue on. "They must've slipped something into my drink. I couldn't move. I couldn't stop them. I tried to, but I just couldn't." Now I'm sobbing.

"Who?" Michael demands.

"Trevor, and some of the other football players. Whatever they gave me caused me to black out, so I don't know who all was there."

"How... why?" Michael starts. I don't want to say it. I don't want him to blame himself. It wasn't his fault. He wasn't one of the evil monsters who assaulted me that night. When I just look at him with a sympathetic glance, he seems to understand. "Because of me?" Michael asks, suddenly looking crestfallen. "Shit, Grace... Why didn't you ever tell me?"

"Because football made you happy. I couldn't tell you. You would've quit the team or retaliated. You were already dealing with so much..."

"It doesn't fucking matter. You are my family, Grace. With everything you've done for me..." He swears under his breath. "I'm going to make this right, Grace. Even if I have to fucking kill him."

"No!" I shout. "No! He's already ruined so much. Please, please don't let him ruin your life. He's not worth it."

"Grace, he can't get away with this. Why didn't you report it?" Michael asks.

Lisa jumps in. "You know they wouldn't have done anything anyway. I mean look at the way they treated you, and nothing ever happened."

"This is different! It's not just some homophobic taunts, this is rape, Grace!"

"I know." I say quietly.

Michael runs his hands through his hair and pulls hard at the ends.

"Grace, I don't know if I can let this go. Trevor already made my life miserable in high school, but to know what he did to you. I can't forgive that. I can't forget it. I can't let him get away with it."

"Michael, I don't want anything taking football away from you, especially Trevor."

"This isn't high school anymore. His daddy can't protect him now. His daddy can't kick me off the football team."

I rest my hand on his thigh. "Please don't do anything stupid."

"Grace." He says, sounding defeated and hanging his head.

"I'm okay."

"But are you? This is why you've been so closed off from men isn't it? It's why you've been so understanding and wanting to continue all of this?" He motions his hand between us.

I nod, not making eye contact with him. He sighs.

"I'm going to figure out how to make this okay, Grace."

"There's nothing to make okay, Michael. It happened. It was awful and it broke me, but there's nothing that you can do about it now."

He grabs my chin and lifts it so that I'm looking into his eyes. "You're not broken, Grace. You went through something terribly traumatic, but you're not broken. I'll be by your side for whatever you need to help you heal. I can't promise I won't punch Trevor's lights out if I see him again though." Michael says.

"I second that." Lisa adds in.

I stand and pull them both into a big hug.

"You two are my best friends. I wouldn't be where I am without you."

"No more secrets Grace, please. I knew something happened. I knew there was a reason you never fought me on our charade, but I never would've expected this. I appreciate that you were trying to keep it from me so that I wouldn't lose football, but I would've gladly given it up for you."

"I know, that's why I didn't tell you." I say.

"Is that why you started dressing differently? Wearing baggy clothes?"

I nod. "I didn't want to attract attention."

He sighs again. "Just no more secrets. Please." I nod. Even though I guess I'm still keeping a secret from him. Like the fact that I want his roommate. I think enough has been shared for today though.

"I'm gonna go. Tonight took a lot out of me." I say.

He nods and wraps me in another big hug. "I'm always here for you Grace." He whispers into my ear.

# CHAPTER 6

I'm dying to be in my room right now. I want to be taking care of Grace, even though that's not my job. She looked so broken earlier. I wanted to wrap my arms around her, comfort her.

I didn't even want to go to that stupid frat party, but I'm glad I did. I'm glad I was able to somewhat comfort her, through whatever happened there. I've never seen her like that. She's usually quiet, and an introvert as she says, but I've never seen her look so fragile. She just froze, her skin paled, her breath shortened. What did that guy do to her?

Lisa leads Grace out of my room.

"You okay?" I ask, instantly regretting the stupid question.

"I will be." She says softly. "I'll talk to you later."

I watch them as they head to the elevator, and then I walk back into my room where Michael is sitting on the couch, his head in his hands. When I close the door, he looks up at me and there are tears in his eyes.

"Hey, man, you okay?" I ask and he shakes his head.

"They fucking raped her man." He says.

Instantly my body tightens from the rage I feel. "Who?"

"Apparently some guys on the football team from high school. Trevor, the jack off from the party tonight, being the one who started it all. They drugged her and raped her. She never even fucking told me."

"Why didn't she tell you?"

"She said she knew football was the only thing that made me happy. She didn't want me to retaliate or quit. Jesus Christ, how can she think that football means more to me than she does? She's fucking family."

When he says this, my stomach sinks. I know it's wrong to want your friend's girl, but hearing how much she means to him tears me apart inside and overwhelms me with guilt.

"Why didn't she report it?"

"You don't get how our town worked, man. Football players were looked at like gods, especially Trevor fucking Donovan. His dad was the football coach. He never got in trouble for anything he did, to anyone."

I sit down with a huff.

"I just don't get how anyone can hurt Grace. She's the sweetest girl there is. She will do anything for anyone. Hell, look at what she's been doing for me all these years." Michael says softly.

"What has she been doing?" I ask even though there are much more important questions to ask right now.

He looks at me, and I can't quite decipher the look in his eyes.

"Nothing, just being there for me, ya know?" He says, and even though I think there's more than what he's saying. I don't push. I just nod.

"What're you going to do now?" I ask.

"I don't know. I really fucking don't. She doesn't want me to retaliate, which I get and appreciate her looking out for me. But how can I not? He fucking raped her. He hurt her. She's been living with this all these years and I never knew. I never fucking knew. How did I not see it? I knew something had happened because she used to be so full of life, and then she started to shut down. She started wearing baggy clothes. I never even thought about it. I just thought she was changing her style or some shit."

Then an idea pops into my head. "Doesn't Trevor play for the Hawks?" I ask.

Michael turns to look at me. "Yeah?"

"What position does Trevor play?" I ask.

"Wide Receiver. Why?" Michael says, almost questioningly.

"Well, we're playing them next week." I say.

I see a smile start to form on his face. "What're you thinking?"

"Well first, we beat them, destroy them. A win will definitely hurt his ego." I say.

"And?" Michael prompts.

"I'm sure the coach will understand a little unnecessary roughness." I say with a smirk.

"I like it. If it's on the field, Grace can't get mad for me retaliating. It's just football." He says with a chuckle. "I've never wanted to be on defense before, but damn, I wish I was on the defensive line for that game."

"Leave it to me." I say.

He looks at me for a minute. "Do you like her?"

"Who?"

"Mother Theresa." He says with an eye roll. "Grace, dude."

"I mean she's a cool girl." I say, hoping I'm controlling the wavering in my voice better than I'm controlling the emotions flowing through me.

Do I like her? That seems such a simple term for how I feel about her, even though it's crazy. Can you love someone who you've barely spoken to? I mean she's beautiful, smart, and kind. Hell, she's even been helping me to study for Psychology when she obviously doesn't believe that I need it. The list goes on and on about all the amazing attributes she has. I can't say any of this to Michael though. Again, I will never be a homewrecker. I also don't want things tense between Michael and me either. He's got enough going on with everything he found out tonight.

He continues to just look at me, trying to get a read on me.

"So you two have been together for a long time?" I ask begging to transfer the attention away from myself, as the guilt tries to swallow me whole.

"I've known Grace basically my whole life. Then in high school, I think it was my junior year, her sophomore year, we got together."

"That's a long time." I say.

"Yeah." He responds. "I offered that we could stop once we got to college, let her explore and see what else was out there. She didn't want to."

That's weird. If I had a girl like Grace, I would never let her go, never even give her that option. I would hold onto her as long as I could.

"Is that what you wanted?"

Another emotion passes across his face that I can't decipher. "No." He says, but I almost don't believe him.

"Are you guys happy?" I ask. I'm probably pushing my luck. He already seems to have suspicions of my feelings for her, but I just don't get why he'd ask her if she wanted to explore outside of their relationship.

"Of course." He says a little too quickly. Something is definitely up. I want to ask more, but I won't. *It's not your business.* I remind myself. My feelings for Grace are wrong, even if they feel right.

"Who's turn is it to take the trash out?" Michael asks, as though he's now trying to change the subject.

"Rock, paper, scissors?" I ask. Yes, this is how two college athletes handle their problems.

# CHAPTER 7

"Grace, we've been sitting here for twenty minutes already, and you haven't started talking yet. Is everything alright?" Ms. Lisbon asks.

"Sorry, I took your advice. I went to a party this weekend." I say.

"Wow. I figured I'd have to push you for a month or more to take that step. At most, I figured you'd go out for coffee not push to go to a party, but I'm proud of you for stepping out of your comfort zone. How did it go?"

"Not well." I say.

"Okay, what happened?" She says as she leans forward.

"Trevor was there." I whisper.

"Oh, Grace." She says.

"Everything came back to me and I froze. I just fucking froze." I say as tears start to stream down my cheeks.

"That's a normal response to trauma." She says.

"I couldn't fight back then, and I couldn't fight the other night. I don't understand why he still has so much power over me."

"Grace, it's because you give it to him."

"What?" I ask, almost angrily.

"Grace, you haven't allowed yourself to fully heal and come to terms with what happened to you. We've talked a lot about it, but I don't think you've truly worked through the trauma."

"We've been talking for two years. Are you saying I've made no progress?" I'm really starting to get angry now.

"No, Grace, that's not what I'm saying. But your reaction shows that you haven't fully come to terms with what happened to you." She says as she raises her palms in a placating manner.

"I was raped!" I shout. "How else am I supposed to come to terms with that? I had numerous boys rape me. Take my virginity, against my will. They drugged me. They held me down and forced themselves on me. I don't even know how many of them because I blacked out. I couldn't even go to the hospital because I knew they would do a rape kit. I didn't want that! I didn't want my mom to have to worry about me. I didn't want anyone to have to worry about me." When I finish, angry tears are pouring down my face, my hands are clenched, and I'm trying to catch my breath.

Then Ms. Lisbon smiles. She fucking smiles.

"Grace, this is the first time you've gotten angry in our sessions."

"And that causes you to fucking smile?" Somehow, her smile grows.

"Yes, anger is a normal part of the healing process. I had always wondered if you had already gotten the anger stage out of the way before we met, but it looks like now you're finally starting to release it."

I'm not going to lie. Yelling, even if it was at Ms. Lisbon, felt good. I feel like I can take a breath after holding it for so long.

"Grace, can I ask why you never reported it? I know we've talked a lot about your trauma, but we never really talked much about why you didn't report it."

"Football players were gods in our town. They could do no wrong. Whatever they did, the school officials looked the other way. Trevor was the worst. He got away with so much because his dad was the football coach and always got him out of stuff."

"I understand that, but no one is above the law, Grace. What he did, it wasn't the same as what he did to Michael, which was awful in his own right. No one should be made to feel like they aren't worthy because of who they love. However, what he did to you was illegal, Grace. He sexually assaulted you, along with some of the other football players. I can't imagine the police would not have taken your situation seriously."

I just shrug my shoulders. "I didn't know what to do. I was young. I felt like I couldn't talk to anyone about it. Again, Michael would've retaliated causing him to get kicked off the team or end up in jail himself. I couldn't take football from him. My mom worked so hard, and I didn't want to put anything else on her either."

"She's your mom, Grace. She may have had a lot going on, but I can't imagine that she wouldn't have done anything you needed her to do, from what you've told me about her. She loves you tremendously."

"I know she does, but I thought I could handle it by myself."

"And do you think that worked well for you?"

"No." I say as I hang my head. "At first, I was numb. I just went through the motions day to day. After I finally opened up to Lisa, it got a little easier because I felt like I had someone in my corner."

"And if you would have opened up to Michael or your mother, wouldn't that have just added someone else to your corner?"

"I guess, but I just couldn't."

"You know you still can report this." She says.

"What?"

"In Texas, there are no limitations for reporting a rape in regards to minors"

I don't know if I can do that. What good would it do years later? I would just have to relive the whole ordeal again. I'd have to recount the details from that night over and over again. Would they even believe me since it's been so long? They'd probably just think that I was a young girl and wanted it or didn't remember the details correctly.

"Grace, you look like you're spiraling. I'm not saying it is anything you have to do, I'm simply stating that the choice is there for you to make."

"I just don't know what good it would do."

"Okay, let me ask you this. If it was Lisa who was in this situation, what would you say to her? What would you encourage her to do?"

I sit and ponder her question. I would go along with whatever Lisa decided, but I would strongly encourage her to tell the authorities. I would remind her that she could stop it from happening to other girls. Other girls. The realization hits me like a punch to the gut, and I'm suddenly feeling nauseous.

"What if it's happened to someone else, and I never told anyone and I could've stopped it?" I say with shaky words.

"We don't know that it's happened to anyone else, and I truly hope it hasn't. If it has though, the blame would not be on you. It would still be on Trevor. He's the one who hurt you. He's the one who believed it was okay to do what he did. He was the one who believed he had the right to take something without your consent. Regardless of you reporting it or not, nothing that has or could have happened after would be on you. I need you to know that."

I nod my head as tears continue to stream down my face. If he did hurt another woman, I know logistically it would not be my fault. But if I had been brave enough to report it when it happened, could it have saved someone else? Which also leads to the question, if I report it now, can I still save someone? Surely someone doesn't do what Trevor did and then all of sudden have a change of heart, or grow a heart. When someone is as inherently vile and cruel hearted as Trevor, you don't just change. But could I be the one to do it? To report him?

"So this has been a lot. I just want you to think about it. That option is always there."

Nodding my head, I slowly rise to my feet and leave her office. The first thing I do is call my mom. She answers on the second ring.

"Grace? Hey, honey, is everything alright?" She asks.

"Yeah, mom." I say as I sniffle.

"Honey, it doesn't sound alright." She says.

"I, um, I need to tell you something."

"Okay."

Then I unleash it all on her. I tell her everything about that night of the party.

"Oh, sweetheart. Why didn't you ever say anything?" She says, and I can hear her sniffling on the other end of the line.

"You were already doing so much, and on your own too. I just didn't want to put anything else on you."

"Honey, I'm your mother. I'm here for you whenever you need me. I wish... I wish you would've told me about this sooner. I would've helped you. I would've done whatever I could for you. I can't believe you've been living with this secret for so long."

"I'm sorry." I whisper.

"No, honey, I'm sorry. I'm sorry I didn't ask more questions when you became more reserved. I figured it was just some teenage girl thing and that you would come to me when you were ready. I'm sorry I wasn't there for you."

"You were an amazing mom. This was just my silly mind telling me that I should handle it on my own."

"Does Michael know?" She asks. She's known about my arrangement with Michael, since she has known him as long as I have. She knows who he truly is.

"He found out after I saw Trevor again at a party a couple days ago."

"Oh honey, are you okay? Do you need me to come there? I have to work but I will switch everything around and be there as soon as I can."

"No, mom. I appreciate it. I promise to come home soon."

"Okay. I love you so much Grace. Please know you can always tell me anything, okay?"

"I know mom. I love you too."

After I hang up with my mom, I'm feeling a little better. Maybe Ms. Lisbon knows what she's talking about. This feels like a weight off my chest. I immediately call Lisa, needing my best friend right now.

"Lisa?" I whisper, trying to hold back my sobs when the call connects.

"Grace, are you okay?"

"I need someone to talk to." I say.

"Of course, I'm leaving my class now. I'll be back to our room in a minute, I'll see you there."

She walks in only minutes after I arrive. She puts her stuff down and immediately rushes over to the couch where I'm seated. She brings me in for a hug.

"Okay, what happened?" She asks.

"I met with my counselor today. I yelled at her."

"You yelled at her?" Lisa asks, surprised.

"Yeah." I smile. "It felt good. I told her about the party and everything that happened."

"Good, that's good Grace. I was so proud of you when you told me that you were going to a counselor. I know people may look down on people who go to counseling because of their skewed perspectives, but I knew you needed someone to talk to, to help you through everything you went through."

I nod. It is extremely unfair how ostracized people can make you feel when you talk about having a counselor or talk about mental health issues.

"She said I can still report Trevor." I say.

"What?" Lisa asks.

"Apparently in Texas there is no statute of limitations on reporting a crime, such as rape, when it's against a minor."

"Oh wow. I never knew that. So what are you going to do?"

"I'm not entirely sure. At first, I didn't want to do it. I figured what good could it do all these years later. What would it really fix? I'd have to talk about that night with the police and then possibly a jury if it ever went to trial. I don't know if I want to do that."

"That makes sense, I feel like there's a but coming though." She knows me too well.

"There is. Then I started thinking about other girls. I mean there's no way Trevor would have done that once and never done it again, people don't just change when they're evil enough to do something like that right?"

Lisa nods.

"So, what if I report it and it saves another girl? What if I can stop him before he hurts someone else?"

"That's a good point." She blows out a breath. "Wow, this is a big decision. I'm here for you whatever you decide. You know that right?"

I give her a small smile. "I know, you always have been. I couldn't have made it through this whole thing without you."

She gives me another tight squeeze. The hug is a promise that she'll always be by my side, giving me strength.

"Can you pass me my phone?"

"Sure." She responds without pause or question.

I look it up and then dial the number.

"Hello, my name is Grace Keating. I'd like to report a sexual assault." I tell the dispatcher, as Lisa squeezes my hand.

# CHAPTER 8

Game day against the Hawks has finally arrived, and I've never been more pumped. I've been pushing myself harder at practice to get ready. Michael has too. I know he wants to beat the Hawks as much as I do. What I wouldn't give for some brass knuckles right now, but I don't need to go to jail. On the field, I can rough him up enough to send a message. And I will. No man should ever take something that isn't theirs or force someone to do something they don't want to do. Trevor Donovan isn't a man.

After the team is all dressed, and we've had our pregame huddle and pep talk, we all jog out onto the field. Warm ups and the start of the game passes by in a blur. I had decided that I don't want to tackle him right away because then it may look intentional, which it is but to avoid any type of serious repercussions, I don't need others knowing that. I'll let him know who I'm doing it for though. I'll let him know exactly why this is happening. How he hurt the wrong fucking person. I make it through the first quarter with just a little bit of extra force when I take him down, but nothing noticeable.

Finally, in the middle of the second quarter, the defensive line is up. It's time to teach him a lesson. I line up and watch the snapper out of the corner of my eye, all while keeping my eyes on Trevor. The snapper snaps the ball, and the quarterback takes a step back trying to find an open receiver. I charge, finding Trevor easily. I put all my weight into the tackle once I reach Trevor. He goes down like a sack of potatoes.

"What the fuck?" He shouts, while wheezing. "I didn't even have the fucking ball."

I grab his facemask and say. "That was for Grace. If I ever see you bothering her again, it'll be even worse next time." Then I toss him back down to the ground. Then for good measure, I stomp my cleated foot on his balls. Trevor screams out.

The ref blows the whistle and calls an unnecessary roughness, causing the team a fifteen yard penalty, but Trevor has to be helped off the field while he holds his balls. Totally worth it. As I make it back to the sidelines, the coach just glares at me. Michael comes up and slaps his hand on my shoulder.

When we pile into the locker room for half time, Coach pulls me aside. I should've known this was coming.

"What the fuck was that out there?" He spits. I just shrug my shoulders.

"Oh no, you don't. I've never had a problem with you having anger issues before. You've always held your emotions back in games, and this was personal. You better give me a good fucking reason not to bench your ass."

"He got what he deserved." I state.

"I better get more than that Carver, or you're getting benched and being sent to anger management." Coach says.

"That fucker is a rapist. He raped someone I know. Someone I care about." I say. I probably didn't need to tell the coach all of that, but if he wants a reason, I'm going to give him one. The last thing I need is to be forced to go to anger management or something for Trevor's stupid ass.

"Shit." Coach says as he rubs his hand down the back of his neck. Then he surprises the shit out of me when he says. "Should've hit him harder."

"What?" I ask with wide eyes.

"Look, if someone I cared for was assaulted in that way, I probably would've killed the bastard. So, I guess I should be lucky that it was just a penalty, and your ass isn't sitting in jail. If you tell anyone I said that though, I'm going to deny it." He says and I nod.

"Okay, I'm going to have to punish you for this because I can't let other guys think it's okay to just take every personal vendetta out on the field."

"I understand." I say.

"You're a good kid. Whoever that person you just defended is, they're lucky to have you." He says as he pats me on the shoulder and goes into the locker room. I wish I had Grace. Even if she isn't mine and I can do something like this for her, I would do it a hundred times over, even if it ended in me having to do anger management or being ejected from the game.

As the second half starts, Trevor isn't on the sidelines. He doesn't return until the end of the fourth quarter. Guess I got him pretty good. Michael continues to have the game of his life, and the defense is solid as we hold our own. We end up winning 48-7. The team starts jumping around, excited for the win, and Michael comes up for a hug. I hug him back.

"Thank you." He whispers. "That part with the cleats to balls was a nice touch."

I chuckle. I'm so caught up in the celebratory energy coming from my team, that I almost miss the two police officers who are making their way across the field. Shit, am I about to get arrested for stomping on Trevor's balls?

The police officers walk past me and over to the Hawks sideline.

"Trevor Donovan, you are under arrest for sexual assault of a minor. Anything you say can and will be used against you in a court of law…" The officer continues to read him his rights as he places the cuffs on him.

I turn to look at Michael, who looks just as bewildered as I am. I turn to find Grace in the stands. I see her with her hand covering her mouth, tears in her eyes, and Lisa wrapping her arms around her.

It's been a long week since the football game against Trevor. Coach has kept me back at practices almost all week as 'punishment.' He said he had to do it to set an example, even if he understood why I did what I did. He didn't want other people on the team thinking he'd gone soft or that they could get away with taking anyone they had beef with out on the field for no reason.

I'm so happy that my class today was canceled, so now I can go back to my room and take a nap. As I walk into my dorm room, I'm confused to see Michael with Dylan, who I think is a soccer player. They quickly jump apart, but their rumpled clothes tell me what I need to know.

"Uhhh.." I start as my brows raise, probably to my hairline.

"Shit! I thought you had class. It's not what it looks like." Michael says as he zips up his pants.

"It's not?" Dylan says.

Michael turns to look at him, almost pleading with him for something. What it is, I'm not quite sure.

"Look, I get that you're not fully comfortable in your skin yet, but I won't be a dirty little secret." He says as gives him a chaste kiss on the cheek. "Call me when you're ready to be your true self." Then he walks out the door.

I'm standing there with my eyes wide, not sure what to say.

"Shit." Michael says as he sags onto the couch and runs a hand down his face.

After a couple of awkward seconds I break the silence, "Why didn't you say something, man?"

He scoffs. "What, that I'm gay? How do you think the team would have handled that? I already know how athletes can be assholes to those who are 'different.'"

I sigh and sit down next to him. "We would've accepted you."

"Yeah right. In high school, my teammates suspected I was gay. They went to the coach to tell him that they weren't comfortable showering around me anymore because I was staring at them. As if, they weren't my type, but the rumors got around the school, and everyone treated me differently. Well, everyone except for Grace."

"So she knows?" I ask.

"Of course she knows. She's always been there for me, helping to protect my secret." He says. "She let me kiss her at a party to dispel the rumors."

Shit. I can't imagine Grace doing this for so long, I mean I can because she's amazing and has the biggest heart of anyone I've ever met. She's put her own life on hold for her best friend, to help him keep his secret, all while keeping a huge secret of her own. I can't imagine the kind of pressure that puts on someone. This also explains a lot of questions I've had about their relationship.

"I'm not gonna lie. I had questioned if you were gay when I first moved in." I say.

He turns to me, shocked. "What? Why?"

"Your side of the room was so fucking clean." I say. Then he laughs, like full belly laughs. I swear I see tears in his eyes.

"So because I'm a neat freak, I automatically like men?" He laughs.

"No man, but you take cleanliness to a whole new level."

He shrugs. "I like things clean."

"Then there's the fact that you're a big hugger."

He chuckles again. "Yeah... I'll give you that one." He says as he rubs the back of his neck. "I've tried to tone it down because I know men don't always like to be touchy feely. Well, not the straight ones." He says with a wink. "Then again, even the straight guys on the team smack each other's asses, so what the hell do I know."

I chuckle. "That whole tradition has always seemed weird to me too. It's awesome that Grace was there for you to help you. I wish you would've said something though man."

"Fuccckkk.' he groans. "I'm sorry man."

"What the hell are you sorry for?" I ask, genuinely confused.

"I kept her from being happy, all to keep my secret. She could've been with you and happy this whole time, but I told her that I wasn't ready to tell anyone yet."

I put my hand on his shoulder. "I get it man I do."

"She likes you too, ya know?" He says after a while.

I turn to him. "What?"

He chuckles. "Don't play dumb with me. I see how the two of you look at each other. I saw how you jumped up to comfort her when she got upset at the party. Then you started asking all kinds of questions about our relationship, the way you took out Trevor, the lie that you were struggling with school." He says as he starts counting on his fingers.

"I mean, she's beautiful, what's not to like." I interrupt.

"Don't bullshit me. You like her. She likes you. Now that you know the truth, there's nothing to stand in your way."

"I don't know man, with everything, it just seems like a lot for her right now. I don't want to push her before she's comfortable. I can wait for her." *I'd wait for her forever*, I think but don't say aloud. "Also, I'm sorry."

"What are you sorry for?" Michael asks.

"I hated the person I was turning into and the guilt was eating me alive. I swear I never would've stolen her from you, I just felt like I couldn't stay away from her."

"Just treat her right for me, will ya? She's special, amazing. There aren't many people like her."

"I couldn't agree more." I say.

# CHAPTER 9



Watching Nolan take out Trevor at the game last week was so satisfying. I'm sure Michael asked him to do it because there's no way that Nolan would do that on his own, right? But watching him being arrested? It was another step in my healing journey. Surprisingly, a few girls at his college have also come forward with their own claims. At first I felt guilty because if I would've reported it earlier, they may have never been assaulted. However, as I continue to work with my counselor and speaking with Lisa, I know it's not my fault. Hopefully though, we've saved future girls from suffering the same fate. The prosecutor has called me to tell me that if it does go to trial, I will have to tell my story. The thought terrifies me, but I know it needs to be done. He stated that with the other evidence they're compiling and with more and more girls coming forward, that he's sure these charges will stick, regardless of who Trevor's father is.

Michael called me and asked me to come over. We haven't spent as much time together since I revealed the truth to him. I know I hurt him by keeping it from him for so long, but he says he understands why I did it. We also haven't talked about the fact that I obviously came forward to report Trevor. I admit that I have been avoiding him a bit, but I've also been really busy with classes, extra counseling sessions, and talking to the prosecutor.

After making my way over to his dorm, I knock and Michael opens the door, pulling me into a hug.

"Hey Grace." He says, sounding extra excited today for some reason.

"Hey Michael." I reply.

He tugs my hand, bringing me inside, and I spot Nolan. The butterflies start swirling around in my stomach again. At this point, I may need a fly swatter.

"Grace, we need to talk." Michael says.

If we were in a real relationship, hearing these words would put me on high alert. Instead, I just feel confused.

"First, I want to you to know that I'm so fucking proud of you. I'm sure it wasn't easy to report him, but I'm just so fucking proud of you Grace."

"Thanks. It's been a lot lately. I've increased my counseling sessions to help myself through it all, especially the guilt. It's helping me heal."

"You go to counseling?"

"Yeah, I've been in counseling ever since I came to campus. She's actually the one who told me that I could still report it after all these years."

"What are you feeling guilty about?"

"Just that if I had reported it sooner, other girls may not have been his victims." I say with a shrug.

"Grace..." He starts, grabbing my hand.

"I know what you're going to say, and I know it isn't my fault, but it's still kind of hard to keep the guilt away. I'm working on it though, and I'm doing good, really good, actually." I say.

"Good, I'm really glad to hear that." He says and then takes a deep breath. "Grace, you know I love you right?"

I nod my head slowly. "I love you too." I say but it sounds more like a question.

"I know you do. Hell you've more than proved that these past few years. I will never, and I mean never, be able to show you my appreciation for everything. You've stood by me through everything. You helped me through one of the darkest times in my life. You mean the world to me, which is why I want to do something for you. It's not a lot, and I will forever owe you, but I think we need to break up."

My mouth drops. Is he for real? First, he's breaking up with me, when we're not in a real relationship, and when I've been doing this to help him all along. Second, he's doing this in front of Nolan?

"Grace, we've talked about this before. You need to have time to explore what's out there. I want what's best for you."

"I... I don't understand." I say.

"Grace, I've been selfish, and I'm so damn sorry for that. I've kept you from going out, meeting new people, dating. It wasn't fair to you. None of this has been fair to you. And then after what you told me about Trevor..." He trails off. "I can't keep doing this to you. Even if I can't be with who I want to be with, I shouldn't keep holding you back."

My eyes drift to Nolan, without me even realizing it, and I blush.

Michael chuckles. "I want you to be happy. I want you to find someone who appreciates your huge heart and sexy body in ways I never could. But trust me, if I was straight, I'd pick you every time."

I gasp, my eyes widening.

Michael chuckles again. "It's okay Grace, he knows."

I turn to Nolan, who nods.

"He knows? How? Why?..... What?" I ask flabbergasted.

"He may have walked in on me with someone." Michael says as his cheeks turn an adorable shade of pink.

I grab his hand. "Are you okay?"

"Jesus Grace. I'm here basically breaking up with you, and you're asking if I'm okay."

"It's not like it was real, but I know how much you wanted to keep your secret. I don't want the same things that happened in high school to happen to you again."

"It wasn't the best way to share my news." He says with a shrug. "But honestly? It was kind of freeing. I'm not comfortable enough to tell the whole team yet, but after how well everything went with Nolan finding out, I'm getting there."

I reach over and give him a huge hug. This is all I've ever wanted for him. I want him to be comfortable being himself. I want everyone to see who he truly is, not the mask he puts on.

"I'm so happy for you." I whisper.

"Thanks, but I want you to be happy too." He says with a serious look.

Without meaning to, I glance at Nolan again.

"Give him a chance, Grace. He's a good guy." Michael whispers. "And from what I've seen in the locker rooms, he's got a great c...."

I smack him in the chest to cut him off, which causes him to laugh even more.

"Okay, okay." He says, raising his hands in a surrendering pose. "I'm gonna get out of here, give you two some time to talk." He winks and then walks out the door.

The silence is uncomfortable for a few minutes.

"Thank you." I say.

"For what?" Nolan asks.

"For being so accepting of Michael. He's never had that before, not from his teammates."

"Makes no difference to me. I like the person he is. I don't care who he dates, well, as long as that someone isn't you."

I feel the heat rise in my cheeks. He comes over to sit with me on the couch.

"So this may be a bad time, seeing as how you just got dumped and all." Nolan says. I roll my eyes and lightly smack his arm.

"Haha, very funny."

"But I was wondering, if you'd go on a date with me? We can wait until you're ready, until you're comfortable, but I'd really like to take you out."

"Really?" I ask.

"Yeah. Seeing you with Michael was killing me Grace. I wanted you for myself, and then felt like a complete asshole for wanting my friend's girl."

"I'm sorry I couldn't tell you the truth." I say as I drop my head.

He lightly grips my chin and lifts it so that I'm looking into his eyes.

"Don't apologize. If anything, it made me like you more. On top of being beautiful and smart, you're also kind and loyal. You put everyone's needs over your own. You have such a big heart that you'll do anything for the ones you love, even if it means you fake date them for years, just to keep their secret. You're an amazing person, Grace."

"Thank you." I whisper.

"Speaking of truth…" He says as he rubs the back of his neck. "I have something I should probably tell you."

"That you're actually really smart and never needed me to help you study at all?" I ask with a smile.

"Shit." He says, looking chagrined. "You knew?"

I giggle. "Yeah. I had a suspicion, but then I knew for sure when you corrected me."

"I'm sorry for deceiving you. That isn't like me, I swear. I just wanted to be close to you without betraying Michael. Honestly? It was awful because it just made me want you more, which then would make me feel even more guilty."

My hand covers his, as I try to console him. "I get it. Just no more secrets okay? I've had enough for a lifetime."

"No more secrets." He agrees. "Well, one more, I have really been wanting to kiss you."

"I've really wanted to kiss you too."

He leans in and gently presses his lips to mine. It's tender and sweet. I run my hand through his hair, and it feels as silky as I imagined. He nudges my mouth with his tongue, and I open, letting him in. His tongue softly caresses mine. Then I give a little tug on his hair, and our tongues start battling for dominance.

I've never been kissed like this. Sure, Michael and I gave each other soft pecks to try and keep up our facade, but we've never made out. That would've been weird, for both of us. This kiss sends fire and tingles ravaging through my body. A soft moan escapes my lips.

He pulls back, his eyes filled with so many emotions that I can't even name them all. Then he presses his forehead to mine.

"Is that a yes?" He asks, and I giggle.

"Yes, I'd love to go on a date with you. I want to warn you though. I've never been on a real date."

"I don't want to push you, Grace. Everything can be at your pace." He says as he softly caresses my cheek.

"Does tomorrow work?" I ask him, as I lean into his palm.

"Tomorrow is perfect." He says as he gently presses his lips back to mine.

# CHAPTER 10

I'm going on my first real date! A month ago, I never would've believed this could be my life. Lisa insisted on helping me put makeup on. I reminded her to go subtle. I don't want to look like I'm trying too hard, also because I never wear makeup I don't want to overdo it. I finish curling my hair and put some product in to make sure it stays in place.

"So are you excited?" Lisa asks.

"Nervous." I say biting on the inside of my cheek. "I've never been on a date before."

"I know, but this is exciting. And it's with Nolan. I knew something was going on between you two. I could see it whenever I was around you guys."

"Yeah." I say, probably looking like a dreamy eyed love-struck girl.

She grabs my hands. "It's going to be great, and we're going to make you look so hot!"

"I don't even have anything to wear. It's not like I bought a wardrobe for date nights."

"I have the perfect thing." Lisa says and runs off to her room. She returns minutes later with a short red dress.

"Um, isn't that a little short?" I ask.

"No, it's perfect. He'll want to rip it off of you." She says, and I blush. "Are you going to get down and dirty with him tonight?"

"I... I don't know." I say.

She squeezes my hand. "Grace, I know I didn't go through what you did, but you can't let those memories stop you from living your life. I would never push you or encourage you to do something that you aren't comfortable with. Just see where the night goes."

"I know, but it's not like I have good experience with all that, or any experience really. The only time was..."

"I know. I know." Lisa says and squeezes my hand again. "It isn't always like that though."

I gape at her. "How would you know?"

"I'm not as innocent as you may think." She says with a wink.

"You've had sex?" I ask, somewhat hurt that she never told me.

"Only a couple of times." She says. "I didn't know how to tell you because of what you went through. I didn't want it to seem like I was rubbing it in your face or something."

"I know you would never do that." I say.

"Anyways, enough about me. We can talk about my sex life another time. I just wanted to say that it can actually make you feel really good." She says with a shrug. "Now put this on."

I put the dress on, and it fits me like a glove. I may be small, but I typically cover myself in larger clothes to not draw attention. This dress will definitely demand attention. It causes my boobs to look bigger than I thought they were, spilling out of the top a little. It clings to my hips, and when I look at the back, it makes my ass look fantastic.

"Damn girl, you look amazing!" Lisa squeals. "Now, go get your man."

Nolan knocks on the door a couple minutes later. I wipe my sweaty palms on the dress and try to calm my nerves.

"Are you going to open the door or make the poor guy wait outside all night?" Lisa teases.

I walk over to the door and open it. Nolan's eyes darken a little as he scans my body. It doesn't make me feel uncomfortable. It makes me feel desired and sends so many emotions running through me.

"Wow Grace, just wow." Nolan says.

"You don't look too bad yourself." I say as I give him a once over. He's wearing those dark jeans that make his ass look so good. He's wearing a dark gray button up shirt, and his dark hair is a little disheveled.

"Ready to go?" I ask.

He swallows hard and nods. Extending his hand for mine. I put my hand in his and follow him to his car. He takes us to a local Mexican restaurant. When we arrive, I turn to look at him, with tears in my eyes.

"You remembered that I like Mexican food?" I ask.

"I remember everything about you Grace." He says as he reaches for my hand to lead me inside. The hostess seats us quickly, and we order.

"So have you figured out what you want to major in, what you want to do?" He asks.

"Yeah. I want to help people. People who may have been in similar situations to mine. Either a caseworker for a sexual assault agency or maybe a counselor. I'll have to look into both options a bit more. I just know I wouldn't have made it through everything without Ms. Lisbon, my counselor."

"That's amazing. I think you'd be great at that. You're so kind and have shown that you're always willing to help others." He says with a soft smile.

Our food arrives and we continue making small talk about everything and nothing while we eat. It isn't uncomfortable. If anything, I feel relaxed. I typically only feel this way around Michael and Lisa.

"So other than a job with helping people. What else do you want out of life?" Nolan asks at some point during our meals.

"Funny you should ask that. My counselor told me that I really needed to think about what I wanted for my life. We had talked that eventually my agreement with Michael would end, and I would need to figure out what to do next."

"And have you thought about it?"

"I have, and I guess it's kind of a cliche, but I want a family. I want a loving husband, kids. Not necessarily a house with a white picket fence, but yeah."

"Nothing wrong with wanting that, even if it's a cliche as you say."

"What about you? Do you ever see yourself settling down, having kids and all that?" The words are out of my mouth and then I feel my cheeks heat up. "Oh my gosh, I'm so sorry. I know I haven't been on a date before, but even I know that is probably a no go for first date topics."

He chuckles and reaches across the table to grab my hand. "It's okay, I asked you first. And yes, I want to settle down and have kids. I never thought much about it before because I hadn't found anyone that made that dream seem possible."

I'm almost scared to ask, but I do. "And now you have?"

"I think I just may have." He says with a smile, that makes him look even sexier, if that's possible. "You know my mom told me that sometimes people come into our lives and we can either realize that we're meant to find something better for us elsewhere, or it just may be the wrong time or place."

"Which one was I?" I whisper.

"Definitely the second one. It was the wrong time for us because I believed you were with Michael. As much as it killed me, I wouldn't have placed myself in between you two if you were both happy. However, after everything, I realized that it was the wrong time because you needed time to continue healing. If I had met you earlier, even if you weren't with Michael, we may not have worked out, you may not have given me the time of day. But now, you've grown even stronger. I'm lucky to be at this part in your life, and I hope I get to continue to be in more of it."

Tears prickle my eyes. "Can you take me back to your place?"

He freezes. "Are you sure? Don't get me wrong, I'd love to bring you back to my place, but I don't want to push you into anything that you aren't ready for, Grace. You're more important than just one night to me."

"I'm sure." I say. He takes out some money from his wallet and puts it on the table. He walks over to my side of the booth and puts his hand out for me to grab. Then he takes me to his car and drives to his room. Then it hits me.

"Shit, is Michael there?" I ask. I know he isn't going to mind, but I still don't want to have to worry about him walking in on us or anything.

Nolan chuckles. "No. He knew I was taking you out tonight, and he said he'd find someplace to stay tonight. I think he's probably with that soccer player I caught him with."

"I hope he can find happiness." I say as we walk up to his door.

He opens the door, places a sock on it, and closes it.

"Presumptuous, huh?" I tease.

"I just don't want any interruptions, no matter what happens." He says.

I'm scared. I'm scared that it will hurt like the last time. I know Nolan would never hurt me intentionally, but the only experience I have is that awful night. He must notice my apprehension because he softly cradles my cheeks in his hands.

"Hey. Look at me."

I turn to look at his beautiful blue eyes. They're shining with love and adoration.

"I meant what I said. We don't have to do this if you aren't ready." He says.

"No.. I want to. I just... the only other time I've..." I trail off.

"Hey, don't think about that, don't think about them. This is your first time, okay? If you're sure it's what you want, we'll take it slow. I'm going to worship your gorgeous body and make it good for you." He says as he puts his hand into my hair and pulls me closer to him.

His lips touch mine so tenderly. Then his tongue teases the crease of my lips. I part them to let him in. His tongue tangles with mine, and the tingles shoot off along my body. I moan into the kiss.

"If at any time you want to stop. Just let me know. I'd wait forever for you, Grace." Nolan whispers against my lips.

I pull him back to me and kiss him again. He starts trailing his hands down my body, stopping when he gets to the hem of my dress.

"Can I?" He asks, and I nod. "I've been wanting to do this since I first saw you in it."

He gently lifts the dress over my head and drops it on a nearby chair. He steps back to observe my body, and part of me wants to cover myself up. The look in his eyes though makes me feel confident.

"God, you're gorgeous." He says, as he lifts his own shirt and drops it on the floor.

I tentatively trail my fingers down his chiseled stomach. He tenses and groans. When I reach his pants, I pop open the button and drag down his zipper. I push his jeans down his legs, as he kicks off his shoes. Once he's in just his black boxers, I step back to take my own look. His body is amazing.

He comes back to me and crashes his lips back to mine. His fingers go around me to unhook my bra. Then he grabs my breasts in his hands and uses his thumb to caress my nipple. I moan into his mouth.

"You're so sensitive." He murmurs.

"It's my first time." I whisper.

"That's right baby." He says. He trails his fingers down my stomach until he reaches my panty line.

He pauses and says. "Remember, we can stop at any time." He then slides his fingers into my panties, stroking my clit. I arch into him, and a whimper escapes me. He gently pushes one finger inside of me.

"Oh." I breathe.

"I'm going to worship you like you deserve to be worshiped." Nolan whispers in my ear. He continues to stroke my clit as his finger plunges in and out of me. Then he adds another finger. Just as I feel my legs start to shake, he stops.

I pout, which causes him to chuckle. "I'm not done yet baby. I just want to taste you."

"Taste?" I ask, trying to catch my breath.

"Is that okay?" He asks, holding onto my hips.

"I've never..." I say.

"I know. This is your first time remember? I want to show you how good it can be." He says and I nod, trusting him.

He takes me over to his bed and gently lays me down.

"Open your legs for me." He says.

I do as he says, and he pulls my panties down. He stares at my pussy for a moment, which I'm sure is wet from his fingers. Then he gives me a soft lick up my folds. I moan loudly, not used to this sensation. He continues to lick but doesn't go where I need him most.

"Nolan, please."

"I know, baby, but trust me." He says, and I do. I trust him.

After a couple more licks, I start to feel a deep sensation building up inside of me. It's similar to the one I felt with his fingers, but it's so much more intense.

"Nolan, I'm... I..."

Then he sucks my clit into his mouth, and I explode. My whole body starts vibrating, and I feel an excessive amount of wetness explode from me. I put my hands to my face, mortified. Did I just freaking pee on him? I should've asked Lisa more questions before I left. Can that even happen?

He gently peels his hands away from my face. "Why are you hiding? That was so hot."

"Because I... I..."

"Because you squirted?" He asks with a smirk.

"I... uh... what?" I ask.

"You squirted baby. It's normal when you're that turned on"

"Oh." I say with a blush.

"It'll make this next part easier too. It might hurt a little." He says.

"Nolan, you know this isn't really my first time." I say.

"I know, baby, but it's been a while for you, and I'm not exactly a small guy." He says. At that, he stands from the bed and lowers his boxers. I gasp as his cock pops out. He wasn't kidding, he's huge.

"Um, I don't know if that will fit." I say.

"It'll fit baby. You were made to take me, and with how wet you are now, it'll make it a whole lot easier."

He crosses back to the bed and kneels between my legs. He kisses me passionately. Then pulls back to ask, "Are you sure Grace? Once I have you, I don't think I'll be able to let you go." He caresses my cheek with such love.

"I'm sure, please Nolan. Be my first." I say.

He grabs a condom, and comes back to place his lips on mine, tangling our tongues. Then I feel his cock pushing into me. He's going so slowly, but I can still feel the brief pain at being stretched and filled.

Once he's fully seated in me, he pulls back from our kiss. He pushes my hair back from my forehead, "You okay?" He asks.

"Yes, there was a little pain at first. Now I just feel full. Keep going, please." I say.

He pulls himself out and then pushes back in, still going slow and gentle. I can feel every bit of him as he moves inside me. I moan, so loudly, hoping that the dorm walls are thick enough so that his neighbors can't hear me.

"Nolan, that feels so good." I moan.

"You're so damn tight, baby. You feel like a dream." He says as he continues to thrust into me.

"Stop holding back. I can take it." I tell him.

He picks up his pace and starts thrusting into me harder and faster.

"Yes... Oh my!" I all but scream.

"Let's see if we can get you to squirt again." He says.

"I don't think I..." I start but am abruptly cut off as he starts rubbing my clit with his fingers.

The pressure begins building again. Somehow, it's even stronger than when his mouth was on me. Lisa was right, sex can feel good. With Nolan, it feels like heaven.

Then I explode. I see stars. My whole body is trembling, and I feel like I'll never come back from this feeling. I feel my pussy clench down on his thick cock, and it sets him off. He grunts as he finishes.

I stroke his silky hair and scratch my nails on his scalp. It must feel good because I swear his cock starts hardening again inside of me.

He drops his head down to claim my lips again. It's just as passionate as all the others, but it feels like there are other emotions swirling in this kiss. Ones I'm not ready to admit yet. We just had our first date and sex for the first time. I refuse to be one of those girls who says I love you after having sex for the first time.

"Are you sore?" He asks, even though he hasn't pulled out of me yet.

"A little, but that was incredible."

"Is it too much to ask if we go again? Because your fingers in my hair are kind of turning me on."

I giggle and continue playing with his hair. "I'm game if you are."

# Chapter 11

Another game day down, another win in our books. We're definitely making it to the championship this year. I can feel it. With my team by my side, I don't think there's anything we can't do. Tonight's win was extra special though because Grace was there in my jersey. It felt like every play, every tackle, every stop of the ball felt more important because I knew she was there, for me this time.

My parents meet me after the game in the parking lot, as usual with home games, and this time my brother is with them. As I start to make my way to them, I'm almost knocked over when Grace tackles into me.

"You did so great out there!" She says as she wraps her arms around me and kisses me on the cheek.

My parents both look at me with differing expressions. My father's eyes are filled with rage, and I swear I can see my mother planning our wedding in her mind. I chuckle to myself at the thought, and also somewhat surprised that the thought doesn't terrify me. I grab Grace's hand and lead her towards my family.

"Mom, Dad, this is Grace." I say.

"Mr. and Mrs. Carver, it's such a pleasure to meet you." Grace says, and then she turns to my brother. "And you must be Noah."

"Grace, honey, would you like to join us for dinner? We always try to take Nolan out after a home game." My mom says.

"Oh, I don't want to intrude." She says.

"No intrusion at all. We'd love for you to join us." My mom says with a smile, as my dad turns to me to whisper, "And maybe explain a few things, huh?"

I chuckle. "I'll explain everything over dinner."

Once we're all seated, I can feel my family glancing between Grace and I. I don't want them to think anything less of her, so I need to tell them the truth. But how much of the truth can I tell? I'd have to reveal Michael's secret, and not that my family would say anything, but I don't feel like I have that right to tell anyone. Jesus, how did Grace do this for so long?

"I'm sure you have questions." Grace says with a smile.

"A couple." My dad says with a chuckle.

"We've heard a little bit about you, but we were under the impression that you were dating Nolan's roommate, Michael." My mom says.

"So, sort of. Michael and I have been friend almost our whole lives. I've known ever since I was younger that Michael was more interested in men than women. However, with how horrible kids in high school can be, he wanted to keep that part of himself a secret. He had always been like a big brother to me, protected me, so I had no problem playing along as a fake girlfriend for him so that other kids wouldn't bother him anymore than they already had."

"Oh my goodness." My mom says as her eyes fill with tears. "Poor Michael, and you, dear. I can't imagine having to feel like you needed to fake date someone just to keep up an appearance, and then you, sweet girl, helping out a friend like that."

"So, what made you continue with the ruse?" My dad asks.

"A lot of reasons. Michael still hasn't gotten to the point where he's ready to tell his whole truth yet, although he approved that I could tell you all tonight. It's not that I'd want to keep things from you, but this secret isn't mine to tell." Grace says. I can see the respect gleaming in my parents' eyes.

"The other reason?" My dad asks.

"Dad." I admonish.

Grace pales a little, and I grab her hand under the table. "It's okay, you don't have to share it all."

She squeezes my hand in response and whispers, "It's okay. If Michael is comfortable enough to start sharing his secret, I need to find the courage to share mine."

She turns back to look at my parents. "It's not a pretty reason, but the short story is that I was assaulted in high school. I've been going to counseling since I started college to help me work through it. I hadn't really been interested in dating after that, so I had no problem with helping Michael further."

"Does this assault have anything to do with that football game where you pulverized a kid and then stomped on his nuts?" My father asks.

I sheepishly grin. "Maybe."

"Sounds like he deserved it." My dad says.

We finish up dinner with more lighthearted conversations, and bid my parents goodnight so they can make the trip back home. After they dropped Grace and I back off in my dorm room, we decided to just stay in for the night. The last frat party we went to was more than either of us wanted to experience again for a while, and I had no problem sitting at home with my girl.

As we're sitting on the couch, I decide to follow her example and be brave enough to share some truths of my own.

"I love you, Grace."

"What?"

"I wanted you to know that. You shared a lot of truths tonight with my family, and I wanted to share one of my own."

"I love you too, Nolan. Even though it's fast, I've never felt this way about someone before."

As I lean in to kiss her, Michael comes into the room with Dylan. His eye is swollen shut and already bruised.

"Oh my god! Are you okay?" Grace says as she jumps up from the couch.

He just chuckles. "You should see the other guy."

My heart aches. "What happened?" I swear if one of the guys from the football team did this to him, I'm going to beat them up myself.

"It was awesome!" Dylan says. "We were at a party and some drunk frat boy came over and started talking shit about me being gay. My knight in football pads here, decided to punch him in the jaw. They got into a whole fist fight. It was hot seeing all your muscles bulging." He says while looking adoringly at Michael.

"Then what happened?" I ask.

"Then he kissed me in front of everyone." Dylan says with a sigh as Michael chuckles.

"You did?" Grace asks.

"Yeah. I decided it was time to stop hiding who I am. I want to be happy, and Dylan makes me really happy." He says as he grabs Dylan's hand.

I look at Grace and smile as tears well in her eyes. I know this is all she's ever wanted, for him to feel comfortable enough to be himself.

"What about the football team?" Grace asks.

"That was the best part!" Dylan says excitedly. "They came over and patted him on the back after he knocked out the frat boy."

"Really?" I ask.

"Yeah," Michael chuckles. "They pulled me in the kitchen to grab me a beer and said that they don't care who I like as long as I keep throwing the ball like I do."

Grace runs up and gives him a tight hug. "I'm so proud of you." She whispers.

"It's because of you Grace. You were courageous enough to tell your secret, and I can see how it's helping you to heal. I'm just hoping I can be as courageous as you. That I can feel free and let that freedom heal some of the past trauma." Michael says, as he squeezes her tighter.

"So, no more secrets?" Grace asks, as she grabs for my hand.

"No more secrets." Michael replies, as he takes a hold of Dylan's hand.

# EPILOGUE



Moving my tassel on my cap to the other side, I make my way across the stage for graduation. The past two years have been a chaotic but beautiful journey.

Nolan got drafted into the NFL for Dallas, which luckily isn't too far away, so we've still been seeing each other a lot while I've been finishing my degree. I've decided to attend a college in Dallas for my master's in counseling.

Michael was also drafted to Dallas. He and Dylan made their relationship official not long after the frat party where he came out to his teammates. They're both happy and living in a suburb of Dallas.

Trevor got charged with numerous counts of sexual assault, some involving minors. The evidence was overwhelming. Apparently, after my encounter, he decided he wanted to reminisce on his crimes and began taping them. Therefore, they had more than enough evidence to convict him. He took a plea deal to avoid life in prison. Instead, he is serving twenty to thirty years, with required extensive counseling.

Once the ceremony is over, Nolan comes up and whispers, "Congratulations. I'm so proud of you. Now Mexican?" I nod, super excited about all of us going to dinner together. We're a large group tonight, my mom, Lisa's parents, Nolan's parents, Lisa, Michael, Dylan, Nolan, and I.

We're all seated around the table, sharing stories of the good old days and recent triumphs. Then both Nolan and Michael clear their throats and stand up at the same time. No one seems to know what's going on as I glance around the table at the multiple confused faces, including the two of them.

"Um... what are you doing?" Michael whispers.

"What are you doing?" Nolan asks, as he waves his hand towards Michael.

Then Michael lets out a little chuckle. "Oh shit, you meant tonight?"

"Yeah, I meant tonight. Wait, did you mean tonight?"

Then the two of them start laughing even more, slapping each other on the back and going in for a hug.

"Does someone want to fill us in on what is so funny?" Lisa asks.

"Well... shit. I wasn't expecting this. How do we do this?" Michael asks.

Nolan shrugs. "I wasn't expecting it to be a competition."

"Rock, paper, scissors, winner goes first?" Michael asks, and Nolan just shrugs again.

What the hell is happening? Why are they both being so weird? Why are they settling whatever this is over rock, paper, scissors?

Michael wins when his paper covers Nolan's rock.

"Yes." Michael says. "You're gonna have a tough act to follow."

Then Michael walks over to Dylan and drops to one knee. Everyone around the table gasps, and unshed tears are glistening in everyone's eyes.

"Dylan, I can never tell you what you mean to me. You saw me before I even saw myself. You helped me to realize what was truly important, and I realized that love, regardless of gender or race, is love. You've shown me what it's like to be loved for who I am, not the mask

I put out to the world. You've helped me grow into a better man, and I hope with you by my side, I can continue to grow into the man you deserve. Will you marry me?"

"Oh my god." Dylan whispers. "Yes, of course."

Our group cheers, and everyone goes to give the couple their congratulatory hugs. After I've hugged them both, I see some other patrons looking our way with looks of disgust. I swear I hear some rude names slip out of one of the boy's mouths. I march over there because I'm done with all of this. Michael was a shell of a person, hiding himself for the appeasement of others. He now has Dylan, who has made him better and brought back the life inside of him. I will not let anyone dull that again.

"Got a problem with love?" I ask the two obviously younger college boys.

"Yeah, when it's with two…" They start.

"Don't you dare finish that statement with a derogatory term." I snap.

"Dero… what?" One of the asks.

I shake my head. I want to insult him, but then I'd be resorting to their level.

"Look, I was going to come over here to tell you off, cuss you out a bit. But I'm going to ask you nicely instead. Please don't judge other people based off of what they look like, who they love, or anything like that. You have no idea what other people have been through and just one negative comment could be enough to ruin their day or life. Put yourself in someone else's shoes. If being with a woman was looked at as "socially unacceptable" would you change who you were?" I ask them, and they both shake their heads.

"Do better, be better." I say as I turn back to our table, which apparently heard my whole conversation because they're all looking at me.

Nolan walks up to me and bring me in for a hug. "You were amazing. You're going to be a great counselor."

"Thanks." I say.

He takes my hand to lead me back to the table. Before we get there though, he kneels down on one knee.

"What are you doing?"

"Well, beautiful, it's my turn."

"You rock, paper, scissored to see who'd get to propose first?" I ask.

Nolan looks to Michael, and they both shrug.

"Can I continue?" Nolan teases.

I nod, trying to keep the tears from streaming down my face and ruining my mascara.

"Grace. These past two years have been the best of my life. I knew from the beginning that you were beautiful and smart. Knowing you now, I know you're kind, loyal, brave, and strong, so fucking strong. You continue to surprise and inspire me every day. When I first met you, I was heartbroken thinking that you were in love with someone else. I didn't know if I should let you go, and break my own heart in the process, or wait to see if it just wasn't the right time. Luckily, we got our time. Our time is now, and our time is forever. Will you marry me?"

I nod, and there goes my mascara. He brings me in for a kiss as he places the ring on my finger. Our family and friends get up for their second round of congratulations.

As we finish the dinner, we continue making small talk and joking about how both boys knew of the other's plans but didn't realize it was tonight. Our family and friends trickle out slowly, leaving Michael, Dylan, Nolan and me.

As the four of us are making our way out, I see one of the college kids from earlier standing by the exit door.

"Hey, I just wanted to say I'm sorry for earlier." He says, which is definitely not what I was expecting.

"Um.." Michael says.

"The truth is that I'm bisexual, and I've never been comfortable enough to come out to my friends about it. I overcompensate and make homophobic taunts and remarks. I'm really sorry though. I should know better. I know how much those words hurt. I'm glad you found love; it gives me hope." Then he looks at me. "I'll be better." He says with a little smile as he tips his head in a farewell greeting and walks out the door.

I turn to Michael who looks back at me with a smile. "Well Grace, I found my love." He says looking adoringly at Dylan.

I turn to look at Nolan, and my heart squeezes, butterflies fluttering around. "And I found mine."

# Also by Rachelle Valentine

<u>Standalones:</u>

Rectify

<u>Sons of Olympus Series:</u>

Sons of Olympus Zeus

Sons of Olympus Poseidon

Sons of Olympus Ares

Sons of Olympus Hades

Sons of Olympus Hermes

Sons of Olympus Apollo

Sons of Olympus Complete Series